SALSA

Written by/Escrito por Lillian Colón-Vilá

Illustrated by/Ilustrado por Roberta Collier-Morales

PIÑATA BOOKS

PIÑATA BOOKS
HOUSTON, TEXAS
1998

This volume is made possible through grants from the National Endowment for the Arts (a federal agency), Andrew W. Mellon Foundation, the Lila Wallace-Reader's Digest Fund and the City of Houston through the Houston Arts Alliance.

Piñata Books are full of surprises!

Piñata Books
An Imprint of Arte Público Press
University of Houston
4902 Gulf Fwy, Bldg 19, Rm 100
Houston, Texas 77204-2004

Illustrations by Roberta Collier-Morales

Cover design by James F. Brisson

Colón-Vilá, Lillian.
    Salsa / by Lillian Colón-Vilá; and illustrated by Roberta Collier-Morales.
        p.   cm.
    English and Spanish.
    Summary: Rita, a young girl living in New York's El Barrio, describes the Afro-Caribbean dance music, salsa, and imagines being a salsa orchestra director.
    ISBN 978-1-55885-238-9 (alk paper) (paperback)
    ISBN 978-1-55885-220-4 (alk. paper) (harcover)
    [1. Hispanic Americans—Fiction. 2. Salsa—Fiction. 3. Spanish language materials—Bilingual.] I. Collier-Morales, Roberta. II. Title.
PZ73.C652 1998   97-23305
[E]—DC21   CIP
                                                                                                      AC

∞ The paper used in this publication meets the requirements of the American National Standard for Permanence of Paper for Printed Library Materials Z39.48-1984.

To Juan Carlos for his unconditional love and support.
To Bette Margolis and Janet Hull-Ruffin for their encouragement.

A Juan Carlos por su amor y apoyo incondicional.
A Bette Margolis y Janet Hull-Ruffin por su estímulo.

Printed in China in April 2015–June 2015 by Creative Printing USA Inc.
12 11 10 9 8 7 6 5 4

Salsa means sauce in Spanish. It is also the name of a dance music.

La salsa es un condimento. También es el nombre de una música bailable.

My uncle José, who is a bongo player, told me that salsa is a spicy Afro-Caribbean Music.

Mi tío José, quien es bongocero, me dijo que la salsa es un tipo de música afro-caribeña.

NEW YORK CITY

PUERTO RICO

PANAMA

COLOMBIA   VENEZUELA

OLD SLAVE ROUTES

AFRICA

My family and I live in El Barrio. My family has been playing and dancing salsa for generations.

Mi familia y yo vivimos en El Barrio. Mi familia ha estado tocando y bailando salsa por generaciones.

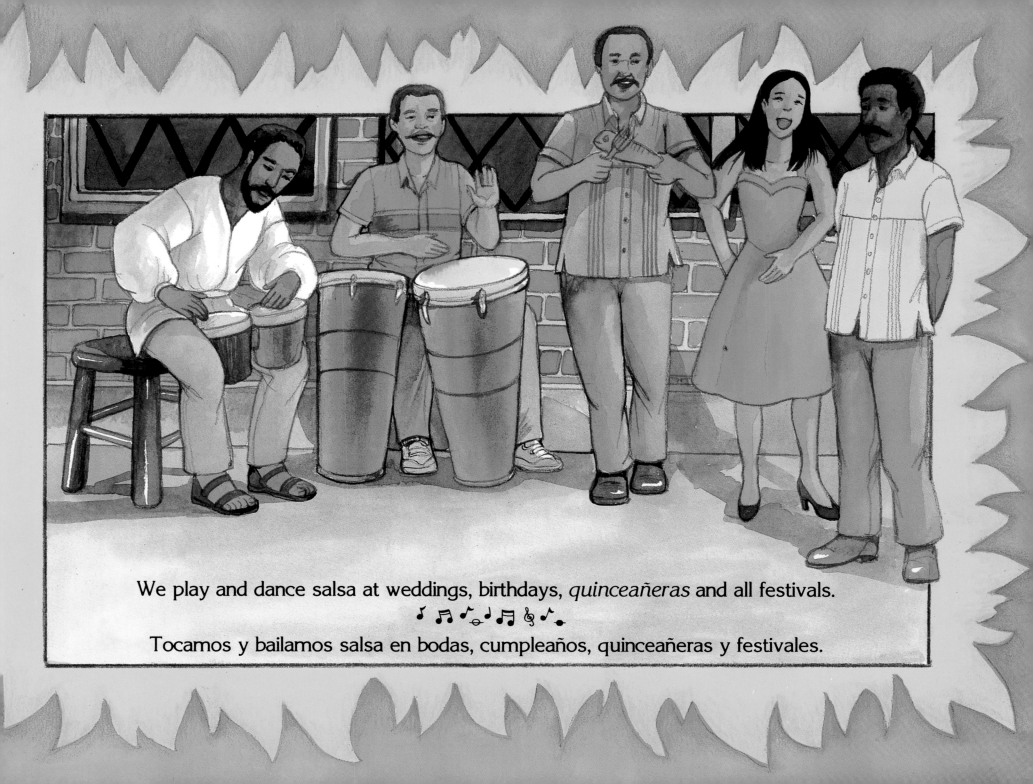

We play and dance salsa at weddings, birthdays, *quinceañeras* and all festivals.

Tocamos y bailamos salsa en bodas, cumpleaños, quinceañeras y festivales.

I enjoy salsa very much. It is fun to dance and to play the *güiro*.

Yo disfruto mucho de la salsa. Es divertido bailar y tocar el güiro.

Sometimes I dance. Other times I
make believe I am one of the musicians.

Algunas veces bailo y otras veces me
imagino que soy uno de los músicos.

Now I'll dance like my aunt Luisa. She says, "Rita, dance salsa with a very straight back so you'll look elegant."
1-2 *cha-cha-chá...*
1-2 *cha-cha-chá...*

Ahora bailaré como mi tía Luisa. Ella dice, —Rita, baila salsa con la espalda bien recta. Así te verás elegante.
1-2 cha-cha-chá...
1-2 cha-cha-chá...

My cousin Diana is the best female salsa singer in the barrio.

Mi prima Diana es la mejor cantante femenina del barrio.

For the time being, I'll dress like her. I'll dance and sing and shake my shoulders and yell, "*¡Ay bendito!*"

Por el momento me vestiré como ella. Bailaré, cantaré y agitaré los hombros y gritaré "¡Ay bendito!"

I'll imitate my brother Alberto who lives in Puerto Rico. He is a great dancer. He spins and twirls. "Rita," he says, "the most important part of the dance is how you and your partner turn around." Alberto spins his girlfriend Rosie until she gets dizzy. 1-2 spin, 1-2 turn around, 1-2 twirl... That's enough for me.

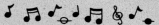

Imitaré a mi hermano Alberto quien vive en Puerto Rico. El es un gran bailarín. El da vueltas y vueltas al bailar.

—Rita— él dice —la parte más importante del baile es como tú y tu pareja dan vueltas.— Alberto gira a su novia Rosie hasta marearla. 1-2 gira, 1-2 vuelta, 1-2 gira... Es suficiente para mí.

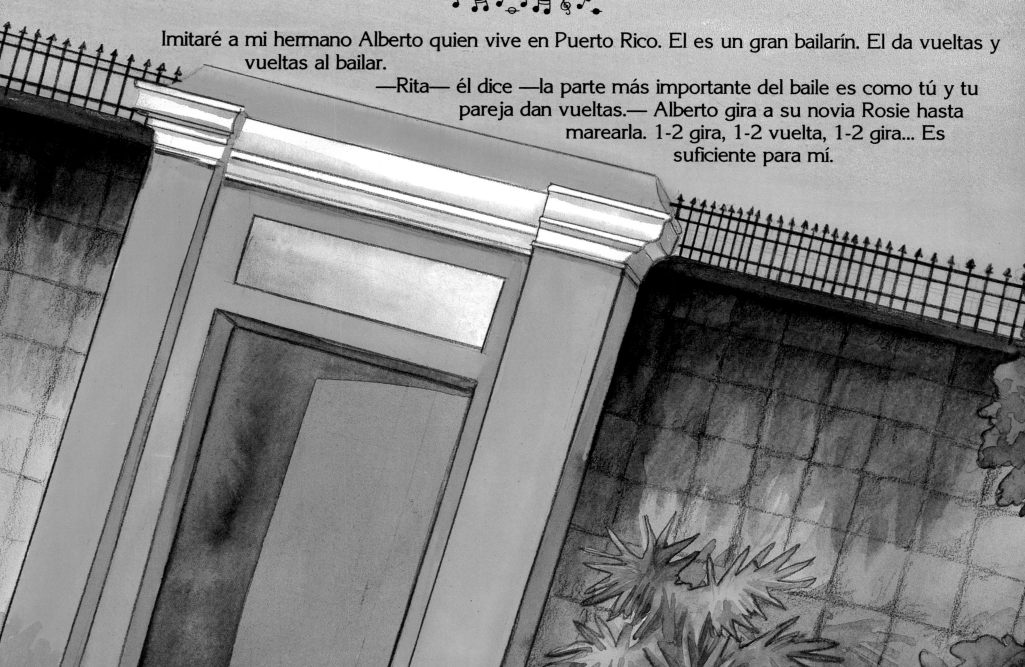

Now I'm my sister Marta. "Rita," she lectures me, "a good female salsa dancer has to dance in high heels without wobbling on the dance floor."

Ahora soy mi hermana Marta. —Rita— ella me asegura —una buena bailarina de salsa tiene que bailar con zapatos de tacón alto y sin tambalearse.

I guess my mom's heels are too high for me.

Creo que los tacones de mi mamá son demasiado altos para mí.

Stretching and reaching for all those peppery Caribbean notes,

Estirando y extendiendo mis dedos por esas notas caribeñas tan pimenteras,

I'm piano player Pedro Pérez, Aunt Luisa's husband.

soy el pianista Pedro Pérez, el esposo de Tía Luisa.

My grandfather, who has won many salsa dance contests, says, "Rita, the most important thing is to feel and live the music. You have to sway your body to the rhythm."

Mi abuelo, quien ha ganado muchas competencias bailando salsa, dice —Rita, lo más importante es sentir y vivir la música. Tienes que mover el cuerpo al ritmo de la música.

"1-2 back,
1-2 move those
hips, 1-2 shake those
shoulders, 1-2 *cha-cha-chá...*"

—1-2 atrás, 1-2 mueve las
caderas, 1-2 agita los hombros,
1-2 cha-cha-chá...

Bum, bam, bum, bam... I'm conga player Ricky Hard Hands. You have to hit the conga real hard, even use your elbows...

Bum, bam, bum, bam... Soy el conguero Ricky Manos Duras. Tienes que pegarle a la conga bien duro, hasta con los codos...

Bumbambum, faster, bum bambumbam, elbow, bumbam. I'm exhausted.

Bumbambúm, más rápido, bum bambumbám, codo, bumbám. Estoy agotada.

I'll make-believe I have a partner. My mother says, "Rita, follow your partner at all times. You'll make fewer mistakes." It's hard to follow a broom.

Me imaginaré que tengo pareja. Mi mamá dice —Rita, sigue a tu pareja en todo momento. Cometerás menos errores.— Es difícil seguir a una escoba.

I'd rather play my trombone like Mr. Delgado, my music teacher. Blow! Hold those notes! Blow until your cheeks explode. Blow and blow.

Prefiero tocar mi trombón como el Sr. Delgado, mi maestro de música. ¡Sopla! ¡Aguanta esas notas! Sopla hasta que te exploten las mejillas. Sopla y sopla.

I'm going to be a salsa trombone player just like my teacher. I already play some of his songs.

Voy a ser un músico de salsa. Tocaré el trombón como mi maestro. Ya toco algunas de sus canciones.

I'll write songs in Spanish and English. I'll have my own band. I'll be the first ever female salsa orchestra director.

Escribiré canciones en español y en inglés. Tendré mi propia orquesta. Seré la primera mujer que dirija una orquesta de salsa.

I also love to dance salsa. I say the best way is to do it for fun!

También me encanta bailar salsa. Digo que lo mejor es bailarla para divertirse.

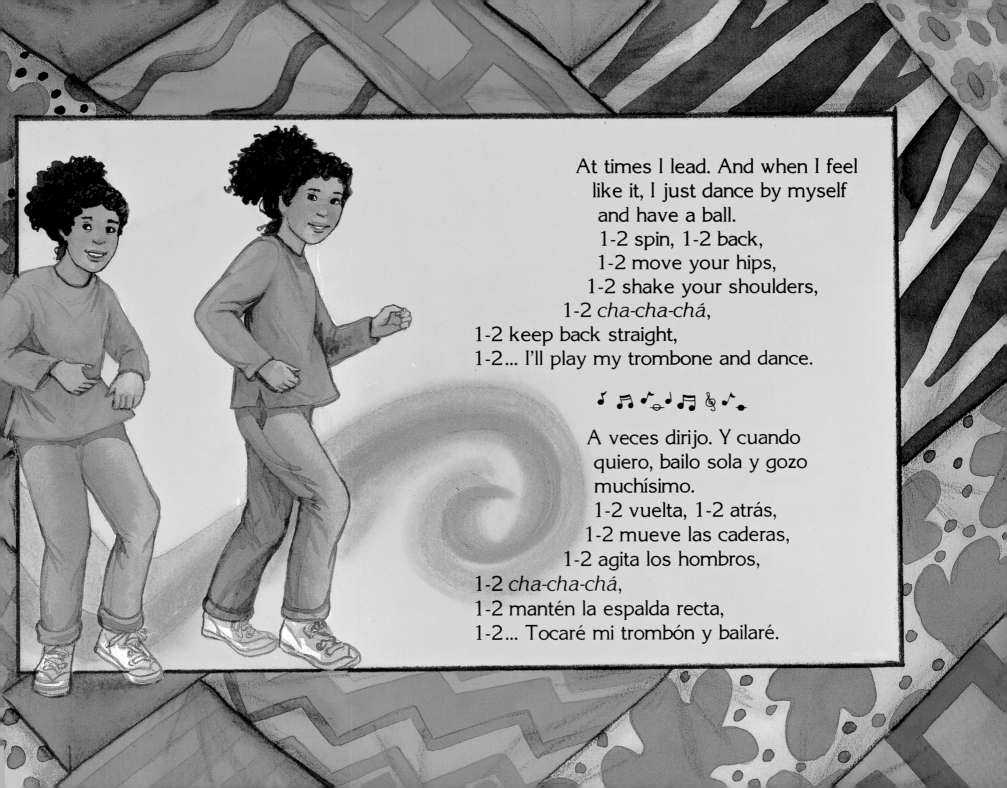

At times I lead. And when I feel
like it, I just dance by myself
and have a ball.
1-2 spin, 1-2 back,
1-2 move your hips,
1-2 shake your shoulders,
1-2 *cha-cha-chá*,
1-2 keep back straight,
1-2... I'll play my trombone and dance.

A veces dirijo. Y cuando
quiero, bailo sola y gozo
muchísimo.
1-2 vuelta, 1-2 atrás,
1-2 mueve las caderas,
1-2 agita los hombros,
1-2 *cha-cha-chá*,
1-2 mantén la espalda recta,
1-2... Tocaré mi trombón y bailaré.

Lillian Colón-Vilá is a bilingual education teacher currently living in Oldsmar, Florida. She has a bachelor of arts in English literature from the University of Puerto Rico and a master of arts degree in Latin American and Caribbean Studies from New York University. Although *Salsa* is Colón-Vilá's first book for children, weaving literature and art is a theme evident throughout her career. She has developed after-school programs for children and workshops for teachers that connect literature and various art forms, including dance, art and drama.

♪ ♫ ♪ ♩ ♫ 𝄞 ♪

Lillian Colón-Vilá es maestra bilingüe y actualmente reside en Oldsmar, Florida. Hizo sus estudios de licenciatura en Inglés en la Universidad de Puerto Rico y obtuvo su Maestría en Estudios Latinoamericanos y Caribeños en la Universidad de Nueva York. Aunque *Salsa* es su primer libro, Colón-Vilá ha entretejido la literatura con las artes a través de su carrera. Es fundadora de programas extracurriculares para niños y talleres para adultos que relacionan la literatura con varias formas artísticas, inclusive el baile, las artes gráficas y el drama.

Roberta Collier-Morales is an art teacher and illustrator currently working on her masters degree at Marywood College in Pennsylvania. Collier has worked as a professional illustrator for eighteen years and is the mother of Christian (seven years old) and Kara (twenty years old). She currently resides in Boulder, Colorado.

♪ ♫ ♪ ♩ ♫ 𝄞 ♪

Roberta Collier-Morales es maestra de artes gráficas e ilustradora y reside en Boulder, Colorado. Ha ejercido la carrera de ilustradora por dieciocho años y actualmente se está preparando para la Maestría en Marywood College de Pennsylvania. Tiene dos hijos: Christian, de siete años de edad, y Kara, de veinte.